SLEEPING HANDSOME

and the

PRINCESS ENGINEER

BY KAY WOODWARD

ILLUSTRATED BY JO DE RUITER

picture
window
books

a capstone imprint
capstonepub.com

The original story is The Beauty Sleeping in the Wood, by Charles Perrault (1628–1703). There are other versions, including by the Brothers Grimm.

When a baby princess is christened, seven fairies become godmothers. But the eighth fairy, who is furious at being forgotten, casts a wicked spell: one day, the princess will prick her finger on a spindle and die. Another fairy is able to soften the spell: the princess will not die. Instead, she will fall asleep for a hundred years. The only thing that will wake her is a prince's kiss. Years later, the wicked fairy's spell comes true. The princess pricks her finger and falls asleep. The kind fairy, who arrives in a chariot pulled by dragons, puts everyone else to sleep, too. (If the princess woke alone, she might be very frightened.) Then she hides the castle behind trees, brambles, and thorns. A hundred years later, a prince does arrive, the princess awakes, and then they get married.

Sleeping Handsome and the Princess Engineer is published by Picture Window Books
A Capstone Imprint
1710 Roe Crest Drive
Nor th Mankato, Minnesota 56003
www.capstonepub.com

Library of Congress Cataloging-in-Publication Data
Cataloging-in-publication information is on file with the Library of Congress.
ISBN 978-1-4795-8615-8 (hardback)
ISBN 978-1-4795-8753-7 (paperback)
ISBN 978-1-4795-8749-0 (paper-over-board)
ISBN 978-1-4795-8757-5 (ebook)

Editor: James Benefield
Designer: Richard Parker

Printed and bound in the United States of America by Corporate Graphics

THE KING
AND QUEEN

PRINCE
HANDSOME

MAYOR
OOH LA LA

MINISTER
BOING

PRINCE
CACOA

PRESIDENT
NONSENSE

THE CASTLE
MAGICIAN

PRINCE JAMES
OF THE KINGDOM
NEXT DOOR

PRINCESS ANYA,
THE PRINCESS
ENGINEER

One day, in a kingdom not so far away,
a king and queen had a baby boy.
The prince was so HANDSOME that
everyone smiled when they saw him…

… even the grumpy TV
reporter camped outside the
castle. He reported every
single thing the new prince
did. Even royal burps.

The prince was named
Jack, but everyone
called him
Prince Handsome.
Because he was.

The **KING AND QUEEN** decided to throw
a splendid *party* at the castle for the prince. There
were cakes of all colors and ice creams of all flavors.
Important people from every kingdom brought
amazing gifts.

"I bring boxes of *beauty potions*," said the mayor of Ooh La La, "so the prince will stay forever handsome."

"I bring a *trampoline*," said Minister Boing, "to keep him fit."

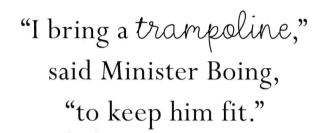

MMM... CHOCOLATE.

"And I bring a bazillion bars of *chocolate!*" said the prince of Cocoa, helping himself to some.

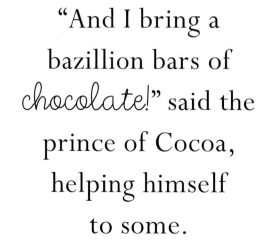

Just then, President Nonsense—
a WIZARD in his spare time— appeared in a
puff of smoke. He was FURIOUS that no
one had told him about the party.

"Oh no," muttered
the king. "We only forgot
to invite the most magical
person ever…"

"Here's my gift!" the man laughed, evilly.
"The prince will be allergic to pointy things.
If he touches one, he will die. And so will
everyone in the kingdom. So there!"

Then he ZAPPED
the prince with his
wicked spell and
disappeared with a pop.

"Ahem," coughed McMagic, the castle magician.
"The president might be powerful,
but I can tweak his wicked spell. If Prince
Handsome touches a POINTY THING,
nobody will die."

"Instead," said McMagic, "you will all fall asleep. Only the gift of intelligence will wake the prince and the royal household."

At once, all pointy
things were banned
from the kingdom.

"No swords!" the king said. "No spears!"
He even banned SHARP PENCILS, just in case.

This meant that Prince Handsome
grew up safely to become a top trampolinist,
a champion chocolate-chomper, and,
just like his name, still very *handsome*.

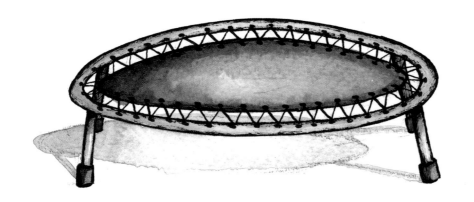

Even so, he was not happy. More than anything else, Prince Handsome longed to be a KNIGHT with a real weapon. People thought he was silly when he fought with cucumbers from the castle kitchen.

Which he was, a little.

Then, one day, Prince Handsome's best
friend found a way to help out.

"Hey, Handsome!" cried Prince James
of the kingdom of Next Door. "Check out
these really POINTY PLASTIC SWORDS
I brought from my kingdom!"

"Wow! Let's fight!"
Prince Handsome said.

But with one poke of a pointy sword,
Nonsense's curse struck and
Prince Handsome FELL ASLEEP.

And so did everyone else in
and around the royal castle.
Even the *mice*.

Over the NEXT HUNDRED YEARS,
a brand-new city grew up all around the castle.
The castle was now hidden behind skyscrapers,
two shopping centers, and an ice rink.

Of course, everyone in the
kingdom knew the story of
the sleeping prince and his
royal household. But they just
couldn't find them.

Then, one day, Princess Anya arrived, determined
to find the prince she'd heard all about.
And because she had been given the gift of
intelligence, she brought along an antique map
and her own TUNNELING MACHINE.

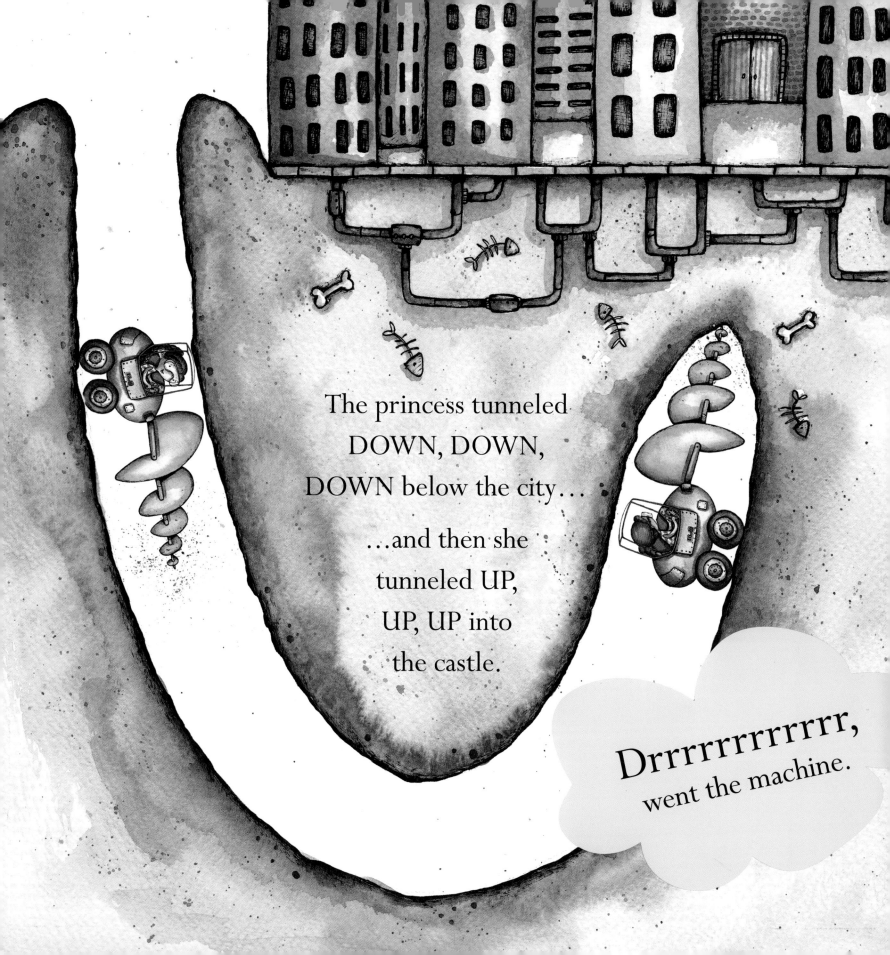

The princess tunneled
DOWN, DOWN,
DOWN below the city…

…and then she
tunneled UP,
UP, UP into
the castle.

Drrrrrrrrrrr,
went the machine.

Prince Handsome was
snoring so loudly that the
princess found him at once.

She tried everything
to wake him.

She *prodded* him.
She *poked* him.
She even *blew* a raspberry
in his ear.

But when none of that worked,
she gave him a KISS. That's what
woke Sleeping Beauty, after all.

MWAH!

At once, Prince Handsome was AWAKE.

And so was the rest of the royal household.

The prince gave the princess a goofy grin.

"You're amazing. Let's get married!" he said.

"Pardon?" Princess Anya raised an eyebrow. "You sent your entire castle to sleep for a hundred years, which is a little silly. And if I married someone I'd known for five minutes, I'd be *silly*, too."

"Oops," said Prince
Handsome. "Then how about
the movies instead?"

"Now you're talking," said Princess Anya.
"I've heard there's a
good **fairy tale** showing…"